# Clifford
## the Firehouse Dog

**Norman Bridwell**

SCHOLASTIC INC.

New York   Toronto   London   Auckland
Sydney   Mexico City   New Delhi   Hong Kong

For Maxwell Bruno Wayne

## Clifford the Firehouse Dog

## Clifford's Hiccups

This special edition was printed in 2011 for Kohl's Department Stores, Inc.
(for distribution on behalf of Kohl's Cares, LLC, its wholly owned subsidiary) by Scholastic Inc.

Kohl's
0-545-35124-3
123386
04/11

ISBN 978-0-545-35124-9

10 9 8 7 6 5 4 3 2 1        11 12 13 14 15 16/0

Printed in China   127
This edition printing, May 2011

My name is Emily Elizabeth,
and this is my dog, Clifford.
Clifford is not the oldest in his family,
but he's the biggest.

Last week Clifford and I went to the city
to visit Clifford's brother, Nero.
Clifford knew the way.

Nero lives in a firehouse.

He is a fire rescue dog.

I asked the firefighters if Clifford could help them.
They thought he was the right color for the job.

Just then a group of schoolchildren came in
for a fire safety class.

Nero showed them what to do if their clothing was on fire.

To smother the flames, you stop,
drop to the floor,
and roll until the fire is out.

Clifford thought he could do that.
He repeated the lesson for the class.

He stopped.

He dropped.

He rolled.

He rolled a little too far.

Just then, we heard the siren.
There was a fire!

Nero stayed to guard the children.
Clifford and I ran ahead.

He cleared the street for the fire trucks.

Smoke was pouring from the top floor
of a tall building. Clifford pushed the crowd back
to a safe place.

He saw some people in trouble.

Clifford to the rescue!

The heavy hose was hard to unreel.
Clifford gave the firefighters a hand.

But then he saw that the fire hydrant was stuck shut.

Thank goodness Clifford was there to unstick it.

They had to get the smoke out of the building.
Clifford made a hole in the roof.

The firefighters were calling for more water.

Clifford found some.

He helped clear the smoke away.

When the fire was out, Clifford made sure that the firefighters got out of the building safely.

They were grateful for everything he had done to help.

We gave some firefighters a ride back to the firehouse.

Clifford was a hero! The fire chief made him an honorary fire rescue dog, just like his brother, Nero.

1. Tape the number of your Fire Department to your telephone.*

2. Know two different ways out of your house or apartment building.

3. Choose a place nearby where you and other members of your family can meet if you have to leave your house and get separated.

4. Never go back into your house for anything if the building is on fire.

5. Tell your mom or dad to change the battery in your smoke alarms every year on your birthday.

6. Do NOT play with matches.

7. Never use the stove without an adult.

*Some phones can be programmed to dial the Fire Department for you. Ask your parents if your phone is programmed and how it works.

# Clifford's
## Hiccups

## Norman Bridwell

SCHOLASTIC INC.

New York   Toronto   London   Auckland
Sydney   Mexico City   New Delhi   Hong Kong

Hic-hic-HICCUP!
Emily Elizabeth sat up in bed.
"What's that sound?" she wondered.

Hic-hic-HICCUP!

Up popped the teddy bear. Up popped
the doll. And up popped Emily Elizabeth.
Clifford had the hiccups!

Emily Elizabeth went down to breakfast.

Hic-hic-HICCUP!

Up popped the plates and cups. Up popped the orange juice—right onto Mr. Howard's head!

"Maybe the vet can help Clifford,"
said Mrs. Howard.

Dr. Dihn checked Clifford's breathing.

"Clifford just has a case of the hiccups,"
Dr. Dihn said. "Sooner or later, they will go
away."

Outside the doctor's office, Clifford

saw his friends T-Bone and Mac.

Hic-hic-HICCUP!

"I know how to make Clifford's hiccups go away," T-Bone said to Mac. "I'll give him a little scare."

But Clifford's hiccups did not go away.

"I know how to make your hiccups go away," Mac said to Clifford. "Follow me!"

Mac led Clifford to a kiddie pool.
"Shut your eyes, hold your ears, then
turn upside down, and DRINK!" said Mac.

So Clifford shut his eyes, held his ears,
turned upside down, and DRANK when...

"Boo!"

T-Bone jumped out of the pool!

And Clifford's hiccups stopped!

"I did it!" said T-Bone.

"I did it!" said Mac.

Hic-hic-HICCUP!

T-Bone and Mac were very disappointed.

"We really wanted to help," said T-Bone.

"You *did* help," said Clifford. "You didn't make my hiccups go away, but I feel good because you tried so hard."

Just then, Emily Elizabeth came by.
"How are your hiccups?" she asked.

Everyone listened. Then they listened
some more.

Clifford's hiccups were finally gone!